DIANE KREDENSOR

OLLIE & MOON

Fuhgeddaboudit!

with photographs by
MIKE MESKIN

Random House 🏠 New York

Ollie and Moon are best friends.
Ollie likes to laugh . . . a lot.
And a lot makes him laugh—especially Moon!
Like when she spins in circles until she gets dizzy—

ha ha . . . hee hee . . . ho ho!

or when she and their friend Stanley compete
in their Funny Lip-Sound Contest.

BBLLBBLLBBLL
BBLLBBLLBBLL . . .

hee hee . . . ho ho . . . ha ha! snort!

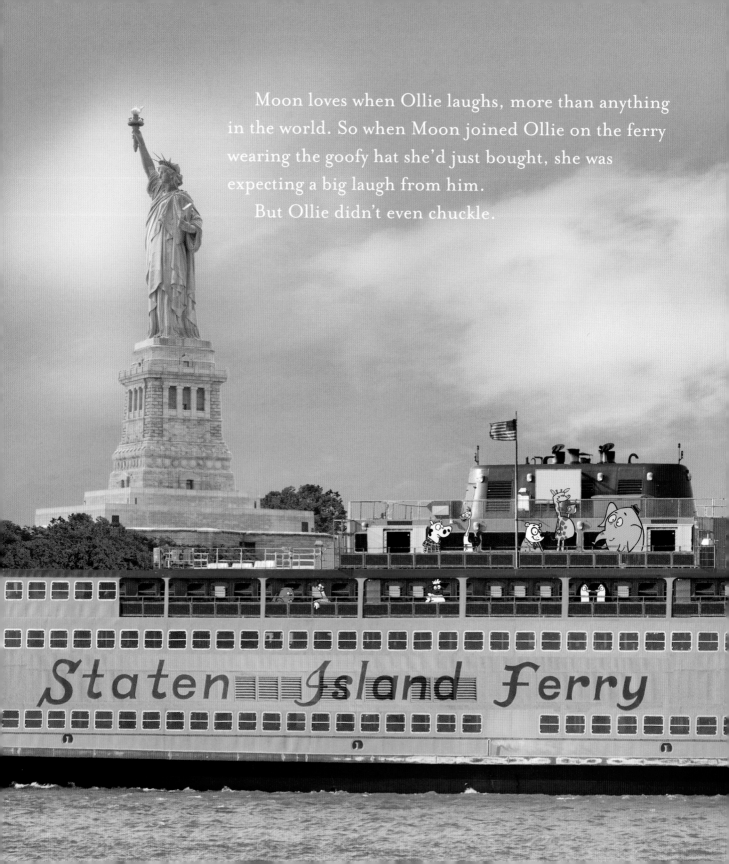

Moon loves when Ollie laughs, more than anything
in the world. So when Moon joined Ollie on the ferry
wearing the goofy hat she'd just bought, she was
expecting a big laugh from him.
But Ollie didn't even chuckle.

"What's wrong, Ollie?" asked Moon.

"Nothing," he said.

"Why aren't you laughing at my hat?" she said. "It's funny!"

"Sure, it's funny, but it's not *that* funny," Ollie said.

"I bet I can make you laugh," said Moon.
"I bet you can't," said Ollie.

A handshake sealed the bet. Moon was determined to make Ollie laugh.
"I have an idea," she said. "Follow me!" And off they went.

On the street, they walked by some food vendors.
Moon searched carefully. "Dumplings, fish balls, chow mei
fun . . . Aha! Perfect!" Moon found what she was looking for.
She held up two fingers to the vendor.

Ollie cracked a smile, but he didn't laugh at Moon's gags.

"Hmmm, making you laugh and winning this bet is going to be harder than I thought," said Moon as they headed for the subway.

Musicians were performing on the subway platform. Moon tapped her foot and Ollie worked his dance moves. Moon never danced. She was too embarrassed by her pigeon toes. *But now's my chance to make him laugh!* she thought.

"Hey," said Moon. "Watch this!" And she tried out a few silly moves of her own.

Ollie smiled and cheered Moon on, but he didn't laugh. So they boarded the train and headed uptown.

They stopped at the library
because Ollie had a book to return.

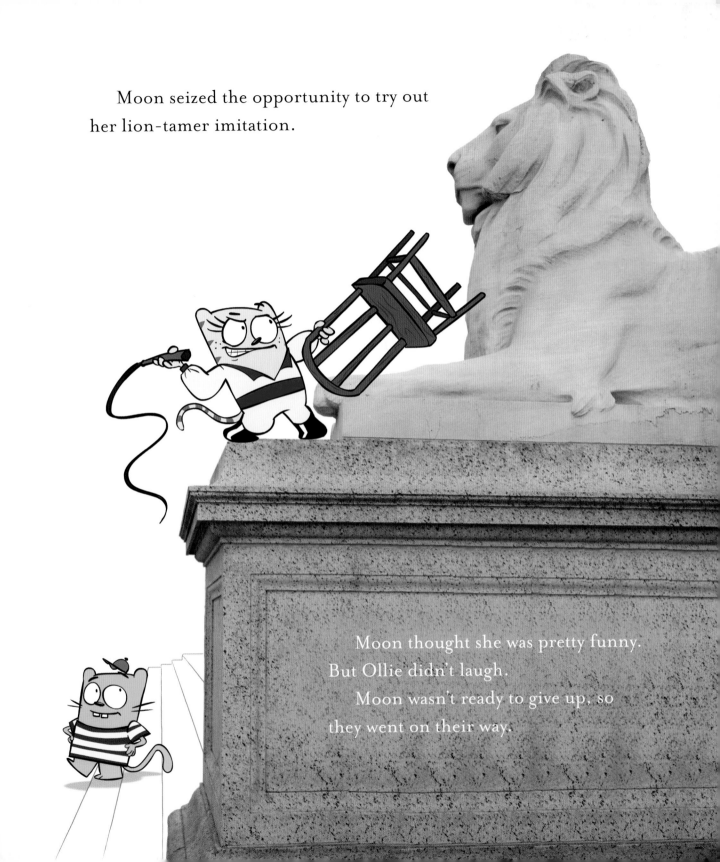

Moon seized the opportunity to try out
her lion-tamer imitation.

Moon thought she was pretty funny.
But Ollie didn't laugh.
Moon wasn't ready to give up, so
they went on their way.

"Stanley?" asked Ollie.

"No, I'm his cousin Johnny," replied the snail cabdriver.

"Oh, sorry," said Ollie.

"Fuhgeddaboudit," replied Johnny, and then he added a funny lip sound: "BBLLBBLLBBLLBBLLBBLLBBLL . . ."

It was the same sound that Stanley made! Moon joined in, hoping Ollie would laugh, but he didn't. He just smiled politely.

Moon had an idea that was sure to work.

"First stop, Forty-Second and Broadway, please!" she said.

Silly snapshots *always* made Ollie laugh!

But not this time.

So Moon decided to call in the professionals!

But the mimes didn't make Ollie laugh either.

"That's it!" Moon huffed. "I've tried everything I can think of to make
you laugh—
   a goofy hat,
      hot dogs sticking out of my ears,
         pigeon-toed dance moves,
            my Siegfried and Roy imitation,
               silly snapshots. . . .

            And I can't believe Johnny's funny lip sounds
            or pantomiming chickens didn't make you laugh!
            I give up, Ollie. You win."

. . . a pigeon pooped on Moon's head.

Sorry!

PLOP!

A split second later, the same bird pooped on Ollie's head!

Ollie started to giggle. "Ha ha . . . ho ho . . . hee hee . . ."

Moon joined in. "Snicker . . . ho ho . . . hee hee . . . ha ha . . ."

They both laughed louder. "HEE HEE . . . HA HA . . . HO HO . . . SNORT!"

And louder. "HO HO . . . AHA HA . . . HEE HEE HEE . . . SNORT!"

They laughed until there were tears in their eyes and their bellies hurt.

"BWAAAHAHAHAHAHA . . . SNORT!!!!!"

"Thanks, Moon. You win!" said Ollie. "Now *that* was funny!"

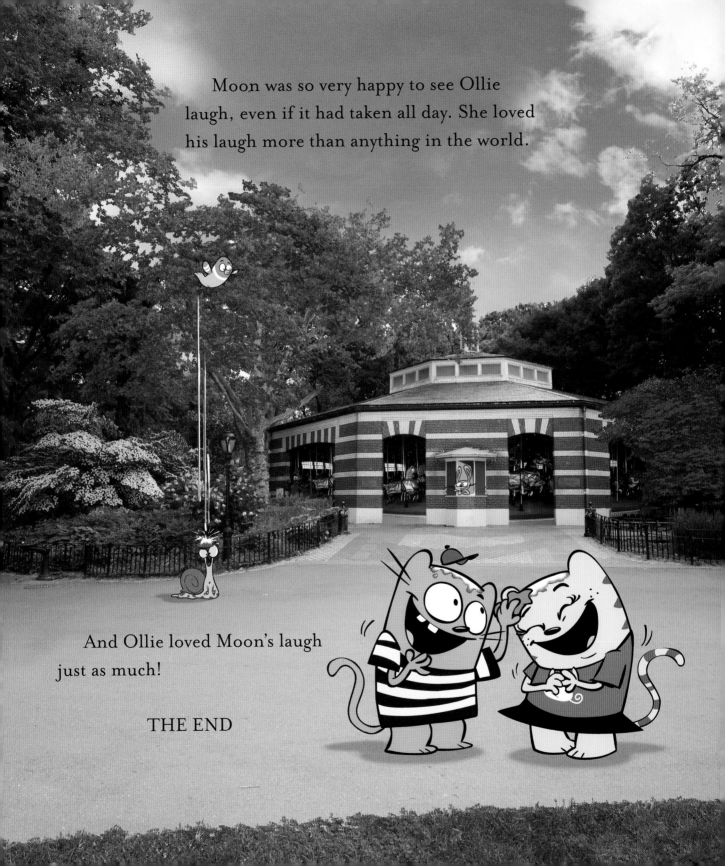

Moon was so very happy to see Ollie
laugh, even if it had taken all day. She loved
his laugh more than anything in the world.

And Ollie loved Moon's laugh
just as much!

THE END